Olympic
Shell-ebration

PuRRmaids

MeRMicoRns®

PuRRmaids

Olympic Shell-ebration

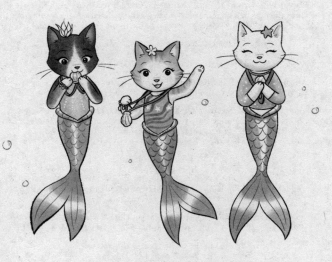

by Sudipta Bardhan-Quallen

illustrations by Vivien Wu

A STEPPING STONE BOOK™

Random House 🏠 New York

Text copyright © 2024 by Sudipta Bardhan-Quallen
Cover art by Andrew Farley copyright © 2024 by Penguin Random House LLC
Interior illustrations copyright © 2024 by Vivien Wu

Random House and the colophon are registered trademarks and A Stepping
Stone Book and the colophon are trademarks of Penguin Random House LLC.
PURRMAIDS® is a registered trademark of KIKIDOODLE LLC
and is used under license from KIKIDOODLE LLC.

Visit us on the Web!
rhcbooks.com

Educators and librarians, for a variety of teaching tools, visit us at
RHTeachersLibrarians.com

Library of Congress Cataloging-in-Publication Data is available upon request.
ISBN 978-0-593-80762-0 (trade) — ISBN 978-0-593-80764-4 (ebook)

Printed in the United States of America
10 9 8 7 6 5 4 3 2 1
First Edition

This book has been officially leveled by using
the F&P Text Level Gradient™ Leveling System.

To Penelope, who is always curious

1

One afternoon, the school day was almost over. In Room Eel-Twelve, only a few students were still working on an assignment. One of them was an orange-striped kitten named Coral.

"Are you done yet, Coral?" asked the black-and-white kitten at Coral's side.

"No, Angel," Coral replied, without looking up. "I still want to fix a few of my answers."

"Leave her alone, Angel," purred the purr-ty white kitten on Coral's other side.

At that, Coral looked up and whispered, "Thank you, Shelly."

"I was only squidding around," Angel said, smiling.

"I know," Coral said, smiling back.

Coral, Angel, and Shelly had been best friends since they were tiny kittens. Angel liked to rush through everything to get to the fun parts. Shelly didn't rush as much as Angel, but she liked to hurry to the fun, too. Coral liked to take her time and make sure everything was purr-fect. The three girls were different, but they still always felt like they belonged together.

Today, Coral knew that their teacher, Ms. Harbor, was waiting for everyone to finish up. Then she would talk about tomorrow's Field Day, one of the biggest days of the school year. That's when everyone at sea school went to Camp Sandcrab to compete in different games and sports. Their gym teacher, Mrs. Furrari, was in charge of planning a fin-tastic day.

Coral loved being outside for Field Day. She loved the sports and games they played. And she didn't really care about who won.

Unfortunately, this was one of the ways the three best friends were different. Shelly *did* care about winning. And Angel *really* cared. They got disappointed when they lost at anything.

That's what made Field Day a little bit less fun for Coral. She was the smallest of the three best friends. She wasn't as strong, so she wasn't as good at tug-of-war. She didn't swim as fast, so she didn't help that much during the relay race.

Coral was nervous when she was on a team with her friends. But she also didn't want to *not* be on the same team as them!

Ms. Harbor swam past and stopped at the front of the classroom. "All right, everyone," she said. "I think we've done enough work for today."

Coral wrote one last sentence. Then she put her sea pen down.

"Can we talk about Field Day?" asked a purrmaid named Umiko. She was one of the kittens in the Catfish Club, along with her best friends, Cascade and Adrianna.

Ms. Harbor nodded. "I need to tell you about the rules."

"We already know the rules," Baker said.

"They're the same rules every year," Taylor added.

"Don't be so sure about that!"

Ms. Harbor said, winking. "This year, we're not going to play some of the games you're used to, like tug-of-war, spoon races, or coconut bowling. Instead, Mrs. Furrari suggested that we could show some Olympic spirit in honor of the Ocean Olympics. We're turning Field Day into the Kittentail Cove Olympics!"

"This sounds paw-some!" Shelly whispered.

"I agree!" Angel replied.

But Coral was confused. During Field Day, all the students were split into a red team and a blue team. "At the Ocean Olympics," she said, "cat-thletes win gold, silver, and bronze medals. If we only have a red team and a blue team, who will win third place?"

Ms. Harbor grinned. "That's good thinking, Coral!" she exclaimed. "We need more than two teams for an Olympic competition. This year, each classroom will be a team. That means all fifteen of us in Eel-Twelve will be competing together tomorrow."

"So no competing against our friends!" Coral cried. *At least that's good news.*

"It gets better," Ms. Harbor said. "The winning classroom earns a very special treat. Do you know who Salmon Biles is?"

Everyone got excited when they heard that name. Salmon Biles was one of the cat-thletes in the Ocean Olympics. She was a champion at swim-nastics.

"Salmon Biles grew up in Kittentail Cove! My uncle, the mayor, arranged for Salmon to babysit me," Adrianna announced. "So I already know her."

"Actually," Cascade said, "weren't you two weeks old the last time Salmon

Biles babysat you? Does that still count as knowing her?"

Adrianna's mouth opened and closed like a fish. But no words came out. Luckily, Umiko patted her paw and said, "I think it counts."

"I do, too," Ms. Harbor said. "But what I wanted to tell you all was that Salmon will be judging a special swim-nastics event at our Field Day shell-ebration. It's called the vault. And Salmon will come back the day after tomorrow to visit the class that wins!"

Ms. Harbor showed the class a poster of the Field Day events. But Coral wasn't looking. She was playing with her friendship bracelet. She did that sometimes when she was worried. *What if I make a mistake,* she thought, *and our whole class loses because of me?*

Shelly asked, "How are we going to choose who is doing each event?"

Ms. Harbor smiled. "I'm sure there are some events that more of you will want to do. And there are others that aren't as popular." She floated over to her desk

and held up a bowl with scallop shells inside. "I wrote the events out on these shells," she purred. "I thought the fairest way to decide your event would be to choose a shell from the bowl. But remember, no peeking while you're picking!"

"We shouldn't look at the shells until everyone has one," Umiko suggested.

"That's a good idea," Ms. Harbor said. She moved around the classroom from student to student. Everyone kept their shells hidden in their paws.

Coral could feel butterfly fish fluttering in her tummy. What did her shell say? Did she pick an event she'd like? Or was this going to be the worst Field Day ever?

2

Coral squeezed the shell in her paws. It was hard not to look at it!

"Maybe we'll all be on the swimming relay together," Angel whispered.

"Or maybe we'll all get kayaking," Shelly replied. "Two of us could be on the kayak team and the other one in the individual kayak race."

"If I'm not on a team with at least one of you," Angel said, "then I hope I picked the shell for speed swimming. I'd be happy doing that."

Coral sighed. Angel and Shelly both loved kayaking and speed swimming. Actually, they loved doing anything where they could go really fast—a lot more than she did. She would rather do something that moved slowly. *I hope I won't have to do those events,* she thought.

But it wasn't just the fast events Coral didn't want to do. The high dive sounded frightening. After all, she was a bit of a scaredy cat. There was no way she'd want to take her chances with something like that. And she didn't even know how to play air polo! She only knew the players had to be out of the water a lot during an air polo match. And that made her worry about her tail drying out!

Ms. Harbor floated back to the front

of the classroom. "Now everyone has a shell," she purred. "Before you look at them, please remember that we're working as a team. Even if you didn't get your favorite event, think about what is best for the whole team. Let's try our hardest to work together tomorrow!"

"Can we look now?" Baker asked.

"Please?" Taylor added.

Ms. Harbor smiled, and the students opened their paws. Right away, there were squeals of delight and some groans of disappointment.

"I'm on the relay team!" Angel announced.

"Me too!" Shelly cried.

Coral stared down at her shell. She didn't say anything.

Shelly said, "You're really quiet, Coral. Is everything all right?"

Coral didn't look up. "I'm doing the vault," she said.

Angel and Shelly looked at each other. "Are you . . . excited about it?" Angel asked.

"I'm not sure," Coral said, shrugging.

Shelly asked, "Have you ever done a vault?"

"I've seen Salmon Biles vault on the shell-ivision," Angel added. "But I've never done one myself in my swim-nastics class."

"I've seen Salmon do vaults, too," Coral said. "And I've read a little about them."

Shelly and Angel giggled. Everyone knew that Coral loved reading. She read every book she could get her paws on!

"But," Coral continued, "I've never done one, either."

The swim-nastics classes in Kittentail Cove taught tumbling, balancing, and twirling underwater. But the vault was an event that was half underwater and half in the air. Coral didn't know any Kittentail Cove swim-nastics schools that had a swim-nasium like that.

"How am I going to learn in just one afternoon?" Coral wondered, frowning.

"Don't worry, Coral," Ms. Harbor said, floating up to the girls. "Mrs.

Furrari is going to give the swim-nasts a lesson when we get to Camp Sandcrab."

Coral frowned harder. "Does that mean I won't get to see any other events?" she asked. That felt really unfair.

Ms. Harbor shook her head. "Not at all. You'll get to cheer on your classmates for most of the day. You'll only miss one air polo match to go to the vaulting practice."

"Good!" Shelly said. "We need Coral to root for us during the relay!"

The bell rang, and Ms. Harbor waved goodbye. "Please make sure you have everything you need tomorrow," she said.

Shelly and Angel popped up out of their seats quickly. "I can't believe we're going to see Salmon Biles!" Shelly exclaimed. "*If* we win, that is."

"*I* can't believe that Salmon Biles grew up right here in Kittentail Cove," Angel purred.

Normally, Coral would be just as excited to meet someone like Salmon Biles. But right now, she wasn't thinking about swim-nasts, famous or otherwise. Her best friends were happy, so she just smiled—but kept worrying. She worried while she checked her bag. She worried while she floated toward the door. It was a lot of extra worry!

3

Every afternoon, Coral, Shelly, and Angel swam home together after sea school. Angel was always in the biggest hurry. Coral had to work to swim as quickly.

Today, though, Coral was barely trying to keep up. After the third time she fell behind, Angel and Shelly stopped and waited for her near the Kittentail Cove Library.

"All right, Coral," Shelly said. "What's going on?"

Coral shrugged.

"Come on, Coral," Angel said. "Tell us. Are you worried about vaulting tomorrow?"

Coral looked down at her tail. She mumbled, "I guess so. I wish I knew how to do one. Watching other swim-nasts on shell-ivision doesn't feel like enough."

"Did you say that you have read about doing vaults?" Shelly asked.

"I have," Coral said, "but only a little bit."

"Well, I think we can fix that!" Angel

exclaimed. She pointed to the library. "There have to be so many more books about swim-nastics that we could find!"

"You're right!" Coral agreed, grinning. "Why didn't I think of that?"

"What are friends for?" Shelly said, laughing. "Let's go find a book that will teach you everything you need to know!"

The girls swam into the library. The newest librarian, Mrs. Bluefin, waved as they swam past the main desk. "Do you girls need any help today?" she asked.

"Yes!" Coral answered. "Do you have any books on swim-nastics?"

"Of course we do!" Mrs. Bluefin purred. "Do you want a book on the history of swim-nastics, or on different swim-nastics champions, or—"

"Actually," Angel said, "do you have

a book that will teach Coral how to do a vault?"

Mrs. Bluefin scratched her head. "I think we do." She swam toward the back of the library. "We just got a new book called *Spring, Don't Fall,* which explains how to do a lot of different swim-nastics moves." She searched a shelf, then took out a book. "Here you go."

Coral took the book from Mrs. Blue-fin. "Thank you!"

The girls gathered around the book at one of the library's big tables. "Does it have fin-structions for vaulting?" Shelly asked.

Coral checked the table of contents. She flipped to page twenty-three. "Here it is!" she announced.

"What does it say?" Angel asked. "Read it out loud."

"*The equipment for the vault is not very complicated,*" Coral read. "*A long swimming lane leads to a large moon jellyfish that is fastened to the sand. Swim-nasts swim quickly toward the jellyfish and do a paw-spring off the top. Before the paw-spring, swim-nasts can stay underwater or leap over the surface. The most important part of the routine comes after the paw-spring. Swim-nasts should spring into the air and do different kinds* of *flips and twists. When the swim-nasts dive back into the water, it is important to land balanced with their tails touching the sand. That is called sticking the sanding.*"

"You already know how to flip in the water," Shelly said.

Coral nodded. That was true. Angel and Shelly had helped her with that.

She was much better at it now than she had been at the beginning of the school year. "But," she said, "I've never done a flip underwater that started with a paw-spring."

"It can't be that different, can it?" Angel asked.

"After all," Shelly purred, "water is just like air. Only wetter!"

The purrmaids giggled. Coral worried they'd been too loud. But when Mrs. Bluefin floated over, she just said, "The library is closing soon. Do you want to check that book out?"

"Yes!" Coral exclaimed.

A few minutes later, Coral was swimming home with her new library book in her paws. "Wait up, Coral!" Angel shouted. "You're swimming too fast!"

"And Angel never says that!" Shelly added.

"Sorry!" Coral said, slowing down just a little. "I want to get home so I can read the rest of this book."

"We're almost there," Shelly said. "But you should save some energy for tomorrow!"

"That's what sleep is for!" Coral replied, laughing.

4

Coral had fallen asleep with her copy of *Spring, Don't Fall*. She couldn't put it down—there were too many things to learn! Every page that Coral read made her feel better about doing the vault at Field Day. In the morning, she woke up snuggling the book. She thought she knew everything there was to know about the vault! But she packed the book in her bag anyway. *I can always read more!*

The three best friends got to sea school extra early. But because it was Field Day, *everyone* was there early! Before long, the sea school students were riding the ocean current systems to get to Camp Sandcrab. The water got brighter as they swam closer to the surface of the ocean. Before they knew it, they saw a small island tucked inside a circle of tall rocks. "We're here!" Ms. Harbor shouted.

Camp Sandcrab was just as paw-some as Coral remembered. The last time she was there, her class had camped out under the stars. But today, instead of sleeping bags, there was Field Day equipment everywhere she looked.

Coral recognized the camp director, Ms. Sanders, by her fluffy gray fur—and her shirt that said CAMP DIRECTOR. Ms. Sanders announced, "Welcome to our

special version of Field Day—the Kittentail Cove Olympics! Please take a seat. Your gym teacher will be out to make some announcements."

Everyone sat down in the shallow water. Angel leaned over and whispered, "Field Day is about to begin, ready or not!"

Shelly grinned. Coral did, too—because she actually felt ready!

Mrs. Furrari was a purrmaid with soft tan fur and dark brown ears. Her paws were completely white, so it looked like she was wearing gloves. She always wore the biggest smile in Kittentail Cove. Coral couldn't remember ever seeing her without one!

Mrs. Furrari swam next to Ms. Sanders. She waved her paws to get everyone's attention.

"Are we ready, sea school?" she asked.

"YES!" the students shouted.

"Fin-tastic!" Mrs. Furrari exclaimed. "I'm looking forward to an action-packed day. We have a lot of events to complete, so sometimes there will be a few different things happening at the same time. Make sure you know what event you're in and when it is happening. Listen for announcements from me or from Ms. Sanders. We'll be giving reminders all day. Does anyone have any questions?"

"How will we know which class has won?" someone yelled.

"I was getting to that!" Mrs. Furrari said. "We will give points to the top four competitors in each event. Ten points for first place, seven points for second place, three points for third place, and one point for fourth place. The classroom with the

most points at the end of the day is the winner!"

"And that classroom gets to have a party with Salmon Biles!" Shelly whispered. She squeezed her friends' paws.

"What are we doing first?" someone yelled.

Mrs. Furrari said, "We have two events that will happen right away. The cat-thletes who will be doing the high dive need to meet by the waterslide. Also, everyone playing air polo, come to the sandbar."

"To be able to fit in four rounds of air polo," Ms. Sanders added, "we'll have eight games at the same time on the sandbar. So if you want to watch the games, hurry to the beach! We might run out of room!"

The three Eel-Twelve students on the air polo team headed to the sandbar. Adrianna was the high diver. She left for the waterslide. Cascade and Umiko followed her.

"What do you guys want to watch?" Shelly asked.

Before her friends could answer, Ms. Harbor tapped Coral's shoulder. "Excuse me, Coral," she said. "My schedule says you have practice for the vault after the

second round of air polo matches. Mrs. Furrari will give the cat-thletes a mini swim-nastics lesson on the deep side of the sandbar."

"Got it," Coral said, nodding.

"Don't worry, Coral," Shelly purred. "We won't let you miss practice."

"I'm not worried," Coral said. "I read so much about vaulting last night, I think I might be ready." She winked. "But I brought my book today anyway!"

"Well, then," Angel said, "let's go cheer on our classmates!"

5

At the high dive competition, Coral, Angel, and Shelly found Umiko and Cascade in the audience. They swam over to sit next to their classmates.

"Is it Adrianna's turn yet?" Angel asked.

Umiko shook her head. "She's going last."

Coral checked the scoreboard. Six cat-thletes had already done their dives.

The student from Room Bass-Three was in the lead.

During the high dive, the cat-thletes started out of the water. There was a large sea sponge attached to the ground that the cat-thletes would bounce on to jump into the air. Then they would plunge into the water. They could do a routine of flips or twists on their way down. They were scored on how good that routine looked.

Coral saw two purrmaids at the judges' table: Mr. Shippley and *Salmon Biles*!

"Look!" she whispered, and pointed.

"It's Salmon!" Shelly exclaimed.

"She's really here!" Angel added.

Ms. Sanders raised her paw and asked for quiet. Everyone looked up to watch the dive.

A cat-thlete balanced on the water-slide. Then he bounced on the sea sponge once, twice, and on the third bounce, he jumped high. A little too high—he twisted a bit too much and landed sideways on the water. Belly flop!

"Oops!" Angel said.

The poor diver floated down to the ocean floor, looking a little stunned.

But when everyone clapped for him, he grinned at the crowd.

"Good try!" someone shouted.

"We love you!" someone else cried.

Coral thought it would be so embarrassing to make a mistake like that. But the student didn't look upset. In fact, Coral heard him say, "Belly flopping is actually a lot of fun!"

"Do you think his class is upset with him?" Coral asked, glancing at the scoreboard. "He has the lowest score so far."

"It doesn't look like they are," Angel answered. She pointed to a bunch of Crab-Six purrmaids paw-bumping the diver.

"I think it just matters that he tried," Shelly said.

As the dives continued, Mrs. Furrari's voice came over the speakers. "The backstroke race will be held near the judges' table at the end of the high dive competition. Cat-thletes, please gather there for your race."

"We can stay here for that," Angel suggested.

Before long, it was Adrianna's turn. Coral, Angel, Shelly, Cascade, and Umiko all crossed their claws and looked up at their classmate. She balanced on the waterslide with her eyes closed. Everyone quieted down.

Adrianna didn't move for a long time. Coral could see her take a really deep breath in and let it out. Suddenly, she bounced on the sea sponge and leapt into the air. She did three flips in a row before splashing into the water. Unlike the belly flopper, Adrianna hit the water with her paws pointing down. When she stopped moving, she threw her paws up and smiled so hard that Coral worried her face would crack!

The judges at the table held up their scorecards. Adrianna won!

"Ten points for Room Eel-Twelve!" Ms. Sanders announced. She started reading out the other winners. But Coral's classmates weren't listening. They had crowded around Adrianna and were congratulating her. Adrianna looked happier than Coral had ever seen her.

"What a great start to

the Kittentail Cove Olympics!" Angel said.

"And look!" Shelly purred. She pointed to the scoreboard. "Our air polo team made it to the next round!"

"We really might be on our way to winning!" Angel replied.

"Maybe we are!" Coral said.

In the backstroke race, sixteen cat-thletes would swim from the starting line all the way to a coral barrier that Ms. Sanders set up. Then they would swim all the way back. Coral saw her classmate Maren waiting for the race to begin. "You can do it, Maren!" she shouted.

Mr. Shippley yelled, "GO!"

The racers started to move.

Maren fell behind almost immediately. So Coral cheered even louder. "We believe in you, Maren!"

Maybe Maren heard her. As Coral yelled her name, Maren moved from last place into tenth place—and then into third place!

The racers had all reached the barrier and turned back around. Coral, Angel, and Shelly kept cheering for their classmate. Maren moved into second place. "She might win!" Shelly squealed.

"Even second place gets our class seven points," Angel said.

But Maren seemed to get tired. She dropped from second place to third, and then to fourth. "We still get a point for fourth place," Shelly said.

Just as Shelly said that, another racer edged past Maren. The race was over, and Maren came in fifth.

The girls swam over to congratulate Maren, who looked sad. "I'm so sorry," she mumbled. "I didn't get us any points."

Coral squeezed Maren's paw. "Why are you sorry?" she asked. "You did a paw-some job. You went from last to fifth!"

FIELD DA

EEL 12
CRAB 6
SHARK 5
BASS 3

Maren grinned. "I heard you cheering. And it helped!" She bit her lip and asked, "So it's okay that I didn't help us win Field Day?"

"Of course it is!" Angel replied. "We're here to have fun!"

As Maren swam away, Angel whispered, "Plus, Room Eel-Twelve is still in the lead. So it's fine that Maren didn't get us any points."

Coral nodded. She *was* proud of Maren. But winning *did* matter. *This just means I have to do well at my event,* she thought. She wasn't going to be the one who let everyone down!

6

Coral, Shelly, and Angel found a place near the finish line of the kayak races to watch and cheer. A purrmaid named Mack was doing the individual kayak race for their class. Baker and Taylor were going to do the team kayak race—*if* they could agree on who would sit where!

The girls yelled for their classmates as loudly as they could! Mack came in second

in his race. Baker and Taylor decided the fairest thing would be to switch who sat in the front when they were halfway through the race. Maybe it was fair, but it was slow. They finished tenth!

Mrs. Furrari made an announcement. "Listen up, sea school!" she said. "The swimming relay is next. Cat-thletes, please go to the racing lanes."

"That's you two," Coral purred. "Let's go!"

But Mrs. Furrari wasn't done. "Also, we are setting up the vault equipment in the deep end of the sandbar. Cat-thletes in the vault competition, be ready to meet there for a swim-nastics lesson and practice time."

"Oh no!" Shelly said. "Coral, you might miss our race!"

Coral frowned. "Mrs. Furrari didn't say I have to leave now," she said. "Maybe I can stay until the relay finishes."

"We'll have to swim really fast," Angel said, laughing. "Which was my plan anyway!"

Coral couldn't see any other Eel-Twelve students in the crowd for the swimming relay. *They're probably watching the air polo matches,* she thought. *Maren said hearing us cheer helped her, though. So I'm going to cheer the loudest for our*

team! That would make up for being the only fan watching.

The relay teams took their places. Two purrmaids from each team waited at the starting line. The other two waited at the coral barrier. A swimmer went from one side to the other, carrying a small starfish. When they reached the next cat-thlete, they passed the starfish along. The swimmers went back and forth until all four members of the relay team had raced.

For Room Eel-Twelve, Shelly was waiting at the starting line. She was swimming the first part of the relay. When Shelly saw Coral, she waved. She looked a little nervous.

Angel was swimming the last part of the relay. She was waiting at the barrier. Shelly would pass the starfish to Umiko. Then Umiko would swim to Cascade and pass the starfish on. When Cascade reached the barrier, Angel would take the starfish and finish the race.

Mr. Shippley was holding the starting flag. But he wasn't floating near the starting line. He was talking to some other sea school teachers. The race wasn't starting yet! Coral used the extra time to push her way closer to the track.

Suddenly, Mrs. Furrari's voice came over the loudspeakers: "Practice time for the vault is open."

But I can't leave now! Coral thought. Shelly and Angel were about to race. She needed to cheer for them! She *did* want to practice before her event. But practice wasn't more important than being there for her best friends!

It's a race, Coral thought. *It will go by quickly. And then I'll go to practice.*

But the relay race still seemed to be delayed. In fact, Mr. Shippley was leaving with the group of teachers. Most of the cat-thletes were relaxing on the sand.

Coral took her library book out of her bag. She would keep reading until she could go to practice. But she hoped the relay would happen soon! *What is taking so long?* she wondered.

Finally, Mr. Shippley floated back to the starting line. The cat-thletes lined up in their spots. Mr. Shippley waved the flag, and the race began!

"Go, Shelly!" Coral shouted, closing her book. "You're paw-some!" Shelly was moving very fast. She reached the barrier and passed the starfish to Umiko. Eel-Twelve was in the lead!

"Come on, Umiko!" Coral yelled. Umiko wasn't as fast as Shelly. She started ahead, but three other students passed her before she was able to reach Cascade. Coral began to worry.

Cascade took the starfish and darted away. She passed two of the cat-thletes and was the second one to reach the barrier. "Great job, Cascade!" Coral called.

Then it was Angel's turn. "You've got this, Angel!" Coral cheered. Angel might

have heard her because she turned her head toward Coral for a second. But then she looked right at the finish line. And she swam super fast!

Coral wasn't the only one cheering for Angel. Shelly and Cascade were bouncing up and down, chanting her name. Umiko was screaming, "Faster, Angel!" But there was still one student in front of Angel.

"You can do it, Angel!" Coral shouted. And right then, Angel pulled up next to the cat-thlete in the lead. They crossed the finish line close together. Coral couldn't see who'd won!

A moment later, the other teams finished the race, too. But Mr. Shippley didn't announce a winner. Instead, he said, "That race was close. The teachers are going to meet to figure out who won. Please wait a few minutes."

Coral frowned. She needed to get to the vaulting practice! But she wanted to see who won, too. She didn't know what to do. *Do I stay to support my friends, or do I try to make sure I can win at my event?*

The best thing Coral could think of was to keep reading until the race had a winner. But it was really hard to pay attention. Coral read a sentence, then looked over at Mr. Shippley to see if he was ready to announce the winner. When he wasn't, she read another sentence. Then she realized she was reading the same sentence over and over!

After what seemed like fur-ever, Mr. Shippley yelled, "We have a winner!"

"Who?" someone asked from the crowd.

Mr. Shippley grinned. "It was very close, but first place goes to the team from Room Eel-Twelve!"

"Hooray!" Coral cheered.

7

Coral wanted to stay and shell-ebrate
with Shelly and Angel. But she had to get
to vault practice! She waved to her friends
from the crowd and raced over to the sandbar. *I hope I'm not too late!* she thought.
She felt butterfly fish in her tummy again.
Angel and Shelly worked so hard to win
their relay race. Coral knew she had to
be a great teammate and do well at her

event, too. *If we lose because of me, it will be a cat-tastrophe!*

When Coral reached the sandbar, the judges' table and the vault were already set up. There was a line of students waiting to take a turn. Coral went to the end of the line and looked for Mrs. Furrari. But she didn't see her anywhere! *She might be late for the lesson like I am,* Coral thought.

"Excuse me," Coral whispered to the purrmaid in front of her. "Where is Mrs. Furrari?"

The other purrmaid frowned. "She just left," the purrmaid said. "She gave us our lesson, and then she went to the air polo match."

"Oh no!" Coral groaned. "I missed the whole lesson!"

"You could watch all of us," the

purrmaid said. "Maybe you'll be able to do it if you see what we do."

Coral sighed. She didn't really have a choice. She hoped that reading about the vault and watching it would be enough.

Unfortunately, watching the practice wasn't very helpful. That's because most of the cat-thletes didn't manage to do a vault correctly! There were three students who were fin-tastic at vaulting. But they did it so fast that Coral could barely see what they were doing!

When it was Coral's turn to try a vault, she did her best to remember what she'd read in her book. She took a deep breath and began to swim toward the moon jellyfish. She kept her paws stretched out in front of her so she could easily do a paw-spring. But when she bounced on the jellyfish, she didn't bounce up and forward. Instead, she bounced back toward where she started! "Oof!" she moaned when she hit the ocean floor.

Coral was embarrassed. Her mouth hung open. She'd read so much about the vault. But reading about it and doing it weren't the same!

It was hard, but Coral made herself get back in line for another try. She told herself, *I'll do better the next time.* She opened her library book while she was in line. Reading the description of how to vault would help her. Wouldn't it?

There was enough time before her next turn for Coral to read the chapter on how to vault twice. The book said to make sure to be higher than the jellyfish before bouncing on it. *Otherwise,* the book said, *you might bounce backward.* "Aha!" Coral whispered. "That must've been what happened to me!"

Another tip in the book was about using your tail. *During the paw-spring,* the book said, *flip your tail backward. That will help you bounce in the right direction. It also helps with any flips you want to do.*

Coral repeated the tips in her head. When she got to the front of the practice line, she took another deep breath and swam forward. This time, she remembered to swim up before diving down. Her paws bounced on the jellyfish, and she threw her tail backward like the book said.

All of a sudden, Coral was backflipping as she sprang over the surface of the ocean! *I'm doing it!* she thought. *I'm doing a vault!* She twirled as she dove back into the ocean. She grinned—until she slammed into the sand on her bottom. "Ooof!" she moaned.

Some of the purrmaids watching clapped. But others giggled. "She didn't stick the sanding," someone said. "She just got sanded!"

Coral got up slowly. She brushed the sand off. And she felt her eyes welling with tears. She didn't want to cry in front of

everyone. So she darted behind the judges'
table, where she could hide. But she wasn't
alone there! Coral swam so quickly, she
bumped into another purrmaid. "Excuse
me," Coral yelped without looking up.

"It's all right," the purrmaid replied.
"Are you okay?"

Coral recognized the voice right away.
"Salmon Biles!"

8

"You know who I am," Salmon said.

"Of course I do!" Coral exclaimed. "I'm one of your biggest fans!"

Salmon smiled. "I'm so happy to hear that," she replied. "But what are you doing here behind the judges' table? Are you one of the cat-thletes doing the vault?"

Coral sunk down to the sand. "I was supposed to be," she mumbled. "But I can't do it."

"What do you mean?" Salmon asked. She sat down, too.

"I missed Mrs. Furrari's lesson on how to do the vault," Coral answered. "I was late because I wanted to cheer for my friends in the swimming relay. And I thought because I read all about vaulting, I'd know what to do. But I was wrong!" She looked down at her tail. "I shouldn't have wasted my time *reading*. I should have been *doing*."

"Reading to learn is always a good idea," Salmon said. "Just because you couldn't learn everything from the book doesn't mean that reading was a mistake!"

"But it *wasn't* a good idea!" Coral cried. "I just tried vaulting twice. And both tries were cat-tastrophes!" She sighed. "Why didn't I leave the relay race to get here for the lesson?"

Salmon scooted closer to Coral. "I don't know you well," she purred, "but I think you probably stayed for your friends because you are a good teammate."

Coral shrugged. "It doesn't matter. There isn't enough time for me to learn how to vault as well as you do!" she cried.

"You're definitely not going to be as good as I am today," Salmon replied. "But you've only been practicing the vault for an hour. I've been practicing for *years*."

"I bet you were always good at it," Coral mumbled.

"You'd lose that bet!" Salmon said, laughing. "The first time I tried a vault, I twisted in some weird way. And I didn't even make it as high as the surface of the ocean!"

Coral's eyes grew wide. "Really?"

Salmon nodded.

"But you've always been good at swim-nastics, haven't you?" Coral asked.

"Not at all!" Salmon said. "The best score you can get in a swim-nastics event is a purr-fect ten. Do you know what I scored my first time?"

Coral shook her head.

"I scored," Salmon said, "a one."

Coral gasped.

Salmon grinned. "My coach said it was a record. She'd never seen a lower score in a competition!"

"Why did you keep doing swimnastics?" Coral asked. "Why didn't you give up?"

"Because everyone starts out not knowing how to do something well," Salmon purred. "Where you start has nothing to do with where you can end up."

Coral thought about that. "I guess you're right," she said. "When I started reading, I had to learn every letter first. But now I can read anything!"

"Which is why you were reading about vaulting!" Salmon said. Both purrmaids laughed. Then Salmon said, "I can't teach you everything I know about the vault right now. But maybe I could give you a few tips?"

Coral nodded. "I would love that!" But then she frowned. "You can't just give *me* tips. That wouldn't be fair to all the other cat-thletes."

"That's a very good point," Salmon said. "I didn't think of that."

Coral scratched her head. Then her eyes grew wide. "Maybe you could talk to all the swim-nasts!" she suggested. She looked over her shoulder at the line of students taking their turns at the vault. Most of them were still having trouble.

Salmon put a paw on Coral's shoulder. "You are purr-ty paw-some, Coral," she said. "You understand *sportsmanship*. You want to be fair to everyone, even when you are competing against them.

You're exactly the kind of purrmaid I'd want on my team."

Coral smiled. It felt good to hear Salmon say such nice things about her. But she was still nervous about something. "Would you still want me on your team," she asked, "if I ended up doing really badly at my event?"

Salmon gave Coral's shoulder a squeeze. "When someone is a good teammate and tries their best," she purred, "I don't care how they score. And I purr-omise, no one else on a good team does, either."

9

Coral and Salmon floated back to the practice line. Coral asked, "Does anyone want another quick lesson in vaulting from a famous swim-nast?"

Everyone said yes! So Salmon started to show them what to do. "Don't worry about going too fast or being too fancy when you start," Salmon said. "Go slow at first and try to stick the sanding."

The cat-thletes did some more practice

vaults. Salmon watched and gave some tips. Coral tried to listen to everything Salmon said. It was all good advice!

Before practice time was over, Mrs. Furrari made another announcement. "Here's an update on which teams are in the lead today. In third place, we have Crab-Six."

Some of the purrmaids in the crowd cheered.

"The top two classrooms are actually tied right now," Mrs. Furrari continued. "Rooms Shark-Five and Eel-Twelve are our leaders. The last event of our Kitten-tail Cove Olympics will decide the winner. Please come to the sandbar to watch the vault!"

Coral gulped. She was glad that Eel-Twelve was doing so well. But now whether they won or lost all depended

on *her*. That was a scary feeling. *I hope I don't disappoint everyone!*

The purrmaids gathered to watch the vault. Mr. Shippley and Salmon sat at the judges' table. The vault cat-thletes waited in line for their turn.

Coral was the last swim-nast in line.

She cheered for every cat-thlete in front of her. Even though she really wanted to do well in the event, Coral didn't want anyone else to do badly.

Finally, it was Coral's turn. She looked around. The entire school was watching. *This is really scary,* she thought.

From the judges' table, Salmon gave Coral a quick wave. Angel and Shelly were leading the rest of their classmates in chanting Coral's name.

Coral took a deep breath. Then she began swimming toward the jellyfish. She didn't try to go too fast, just like Salmon suggested. She bounced off the jellyfish with her paws and sprang forward. She threw her tail backward and did one flip. Nothing fancy, just one flip underwater. She didn't even try to leap over the surface of the ocean. She kept it simple. Then she landed balanced with her tail touching the sand.

"She stuck the sanding!" Shelly shouted from the crowd.

"Yay, Coral!" Angel added.

While the judges decided her score, Coral swam over to her classmates. Ms. Harbor floated by and patted her shoulder. "You did a great job!" she whispered.

"Of course she did!" Angel said, squeezing Coral's paw.

"We always knew you'd be great!" Shelly exclaimed.

But Coral only wanted to know one thing. "What was my score?"

"Look for yourself," Shelly said, pointing to the scoreboard.

"Fourth place," Coral mumbled. She looked away from her friends. "I'm sorry I didn't do better than that."

"You did the best you could," Ms.

Harbor said. "That's all we ever want from you."

Suddenly, Mrs. Furrari announced, "Field Day is over! We have our winners!"

Coral squeezed her eyes shut. She couldn't bear to look. But she crossed her claws on both paws, just hoping the one point she got for her class would be enough.

"The bronze medal for third place at the Kitten-tail Cove Olympics goes to Crab-Six," Mrs. Furrari said. "The silver goes to Shark-Five. And the gold medal goes to Room Eel-Twelve!"

Coral couldn't believe it! "We won!"

EEL 12	38
CRAB 6	37
SHARK	22
BASS	16

10

Coral loved every minute of sea school. She usually went to class excited about everything Ms. Harbor had planned. Today, she could hardly stay still in her seat. Other students nearby began to notice.

"Hey, Angel," whispered Shelly. "I think someone can't wait for school to start!"

"I wonder who that could be," replied Angel.

Shelly and Angel giggled softly. But Coral just grinned. "You're right," she purred. "I *am* excited. You're all going to meet Salmon Biles today!"

"You're going to meet her, too," Shelly said.

"I've already met her!" Coral exclaimed.

Angel's mouth fell open. Shelly's eyes grew wide. "What?" Angel asked. "When did you meet her?"

"Yesterday," Coral answered.

"You mean you *saw* Salmon Biles, don't you?" Shelly asked. "Like we all saw her at the judges' table?"

Coral shook her head. "Nope! I got to talk to her before I took my turn at the vault. She had some fin-teresting advice. It really helped me!"

"You didn't tell us that!" Angel cried.

"We want to hear the whole story!" Shelly added.

But there was no time. Ms. Harbor was opening the door to the classroom. "Welcome!" she said. "We've been waiting for you!"

A moment later, Salmon Biles swam

in. The Olympic shell-ebration was about to begin!

When the students stopped cheering and it was quiet enough to talk, Salmon said, "I had such a good time with all of you yesterday! When I was at sea school, Field Day was one of my favorite days of the year. Even though we didn't do cool things like swim-nastics back then!"

Everyone laughed.

"Congratulations on winning the Kittentail Cove Olympics," Salmon continued. "I hope you're very proud of yourselves."

"Hooray for us!" Shelly exclaimed.

"We did it as a team!" Angel added.

Salmon nodded. "The score was really close," she said.

"Actually," Cascade said, "we almost didn't win."

"We were all nervous," Adrianna said. "My uncle, the mayor, didn't think we'd be able to pull through."

"We were lucky to have Coral on our team!" Umiko purred.

Coral could feel her face getting warm. "Thank you for saying that," she said. "I wish I could have gotten a better score."

"You did exactly as well as we needed you to," Ms. Harbor said. "Thank you for trying something new and working hard to be the best you could be."

"I know this gold medal is for the whole class," Salmon said. "But I want you all to have something you can take home to remind you of this special Field Day." She opened her bag and scooped out a bunch of mini gold medals. "I hope these medals will remind you of what you can do when you work together."

Salmon floated around the classroom, giving each student a mini medal. When she reached Coral, she whispered, "I'm especially proud of you."

Coral grinned. "Thank you," she purred. "I knew I couldn't let my team down."

"Anyone who tries their best could never let their team down," Salmon said.

Suddenly, Coral had an idea. "These medals are purr-fect for our friendship bracelets!"

"Yes!" Shelly agreed.

Angel nodded.

Coral stared at her mini medal. It felt really good to have helped to earn it for her class. *This was the best Field Day ever,* she thought, *because I have the best teammates in the ocean!*

The purrmaids have lots of friends around the ocean!

Read on for a sneak peek!

Early one morning in Seadragon Bay, a young mermicorn named Sirena could not sleep. She pushed the curtain on her window open. It was still dark outside! No one else in the Cheval family would be awake yet.

Sirena fluffed her pillow. She pulled the blanket over her head. But she kept tossing and turning. *I'm too excited to sleep,* she thought. *What if today is the day?*

It was the first day of the season. For most mermicorns, that was just another day. But for all the colts and fillies in Seadragon Bay, it was special. That was when the Mermicorn Magic Academy invited new students to the school.

Magic was a part of mermicorn life. But like everything else, magic had to be learned. The best place for that was the Magic Academy. "I hope they pick me today!" Sirena whispered to herself. She finally gave up on sleeping. She floated out of bed and started to get dressed.

Sirena found her lucky blue top and put it on. She brushed out her long rainbow mane. She put on her favorite crystal earrings. Then she peeked out the window again. She could see some sunlight. *It's early,* she thought, *but maybe the mail is already here?*

Sirena swam toward the front door. She tried to be as quiet as a jellyfish. She didn't want to wake her family. But when she passed the kitchen, she saw that her parents were already up!

"Why are you awake?" Sirena asked.

Mom laughed. "Is that how you say good morning?"

New friends. New adventures.
Find a new series . . . just for you!